ADVENTURES OF
The God Detectives

Nancy Reeves & Linnea Good

Adventures OF THE God Detectives

ILLUSTRATED BY Leslie Chevaliér

WoodLake

Editor: Michael Schwartzentruber
Cover design: Margaret Kyle
Cover artwork and illustrations: copyright © 2006 Leslie Chevaliér
Interior design: Margaret Kyle
Proofreader: Dianne Greenslade

WoodLake is an imprint of Wood Lake Publishing, Inc. Wood Lake Publishing
acknowledges the financial support of the Government of Canada, through the
Book Publishing Industry Development Program (BPIDP) for its publishing
activities.

At Wood Lake Publishing, we practice what we publish, being guided by a
concern for fairness, justice, and equal opportunity in all of our relationships
with employees and customers. Wood Lake Publishing is an employee-owned
company, committed to caring for the environment and all creation. Wood Lake
Publishing recycles, reuses, and encourages readers to do the same. Resources
are printed on 100% post consumer recycled paper and more environmentally
friendly groundwood papers (newsprint), whenever possible. A percentage of all
profit is donated to charitable organizations.

Library and Archives Canada Cataloguing in Publication
Reeves, Nancy Christine, 1952-
        Adventures of the God detectives / Nancy Reeves & Linnea Good ;
illustrated by Leslie Chevaliér.
ISBN 1-55145-542-0
        I. Good, Linnea II. Chevalier, Leslie, 1951- III. Title.
PS8585.E4447A48 2006   jC813'.6   C2006-902450-2

Published by WoodLake, an imprint of Wood Lake Publishing Inc.
9590 Jim Bailey Road, Kelowna, BC, Canada, V4V 1R2
www.woodlakebooks.com
250.766.2778

Printing 10 9 8 7 6 5 4 3 2 1
Printed in Canada by
Houghton Boston Printers, Saskatoon, SK

Contents

The cake reads: GRAND OPENING!

Let the Children Come to Me

"Okay, this is serious," said Fu-Han, his mouth still half-full of cake. "We've worked on this clubhouse all summer and we still haven't decided what kind of club to have."

"We can't decide on the kind of club because we all have different ideas," sighed Tabitha. "Fu-Han, you want a computer club. Jacob, you want a club about dinosaurs. I want an art club. And Emma, you want a club to save hurt animals."

The others nodded. Even though they were different ages – Tabitha was seven, Jacob and Emma were eight, and Fu-Han was nine – they had played together for as long as they could remember, and they knew they would be buddies for life. The friends were sitting on big cushions Emma had brought, eating chocolate cake. The cake was a gift from Fu-Han's mom and had "Grand Opening" written across the top.

The clubhouse was practically finished and it was practically perfect. The only thing left to do was to decide on the name of the club.

Jacob set his plate down. His brown hair fell across his eyes and he brushed it aside. "Fu-Han's right. It's time to figure this out. We can't have four different clubs. What's something we all like?"

"Food," said Fu-Han, as he licked chocolate icing off his fingers. Everyone laughed. "Okay, well seriously, we all like Kids' Club at church," he said.

"I wish Kids' Club went all summer," Tabitha sighed. "I miss it. Although, my favorite thing this whole summer was painting the clubhouse with you guys."

"Yeah, and painting yourself," laughed Jacob, looking at the sky-blue, orange-red, and bright yellow splotches on Tabitha's overalls.

"I miss Kids' Club too," said Emma. "And I miss Maria. She was a great leader and she always told such great stories."

Jacob nodded, "Maria said that when we get back, our first session will be a slide show from the house-building project she's doing in Bolivia."

Tabitha reached for another piece of cake. "Something happened last night that I want to tell Maria about when we start meeting again."

"You don't have to wait for Kids' Club," said Emma. "I want to hear."

"Yeah, tell it now," said Jacob.

Tabitha listened to hear if there was any of the usual teasing in his voice, but there wasn't. Then she looked at Fu-Han, who nodded.

"Okay," she said, pulling at one of the cornrow braids in her hair, which reached almost to her chin. "Dad was reading to me last night from my Bible stories book. But, instead of me just watching and listening, it felt like I was really in the story. I could see myself playing with some kids while my parents and a whole bunch of grownups were sitting on the ground listening to Jesus. There were so many people, but I could hear Jesus talking because everybody was so quiet. Then he stopped. I wondered what he was doing so I looked up. Jesus was looking straight at me. He smiled and I smiled back. He looked really friendly, so I walked toward him. All the other kids came with me.

"All of a sudden, there was a big man standing in front of me. He said, 'Go away and play. The Teacher doesn't want to be bothered by a bunch of little children.'

"I couldn't see Jesus anymore because the man was in the way. One of the other kids grabbed my sleeve and whispered, 'Let's go or we'll get in trouble.'

"Then Jesus spoke to the grownups and he sounded serious. He said, 'Let the little children come to me, and do not stop them.'"

Tabitha stopped and looked at her three friends.

Emma sighed. "Wow. I really like that story. Jesus thought kids were just as important as grownups."

"Yeah, it's my favorite," replied Tabitha. "But this time it wasn't just a story. This time when I heard Jesus say, 'Let the children come to me,' I felt funny inside, like I'd just got off the Scrambler ride at the fair. I really wanted to go to him."

"What do you mean!?" Jacob exclaimed. "We *can't* go to him. We can't talk to him. He doesn't have a body anymore."

"He's still alive, but in a different way," Fu-Han considered. "We can talk to Jesus when we pray."

"Sure, except it's not the same," replied Emma, "because he doesn't talk back. I want Jesus to talk right *to* me."

Tabitha continued. "Dad told me that sometimes when he's praying or feeling grateful to God, he gets this warm, loving feeling, like someone is standing right beside him."

Emma looked at Tabitha wide-eyed. "Wow, is it Jesus?"

Tabitha nodded. "Dad thinks so."

Fu-Han leaned towards them. "You know what? It's not just grownups that get that feeling. Sometimes, I've had the feeling that there was an invisible someone beside me, but I didn't know it was God."

"Maybe it was a ghost," whispered Jacob in a spooky voice. "Were you scared?"

Fu-Han ignored his teasing. "No, actually it felt good. Now I wish I'd said 'Hi' or something."

Emma's eyes grew even wider. "I want to get a message from God like that!"

Tabitha looked at the three of them. "Mom said that when I felt like Jesus was talking right to me in the story, it was Jesus sending me a message. The funny feeling inside me was God opening my heart and my mind. So I paid more attention when I heard Jesus talking to those kids."

"Wow," said Fu-Han. "You got a message from Jesus!"

Jacob balled up his napkin with one hand and threw a perfect bounce off Fu-Han's head. "How do we know it was Jesus? Maybe it was all imaginary." He ducked as a grinning Fu-Han tossed the napkin back. It missed him by a mile.

"This wasn't imaginary," said Tabitha. "I asked Mom how we could go to Jesus now and she said we can go to him by listening for his messages. Like in stories and in lots of other ways."

"That's weird," said Jacob. "Like, I believe in Jesus and God and everything, and I know God came to all those people in the Bible, but that was a long time ago. I don't know if God does that now."

Tabitha looked intently at them. "Mom said to ask Jesus for help, if we want to."

"Okay!" said Emma, her eyes sparkling. "Let's ask him now!"

Fu-Han looked up. "I'm in. I don't want to wait until Kids' Club starts again in the fall for this." He looked at Jacob. "Are you in, Jake?"

Jacob sat silently for a moment. "Ask Jesus for a message? Guys, it's kind of crazy."

Emma began to laugh and threw her baseball cap into the air. "Yeah, it is crazy! So let's do it!"

Tabitha smiled as Fu-Han nodded.

Jacob shrugged. "If you all want to do it, I'll do it, too."

Tabitha leaned back against the clubhouse wall. "Thank you, Jesus, for sending me a message," she began. "We want to be like those kids who went to you, so, um, could you please send us more messages?"

Fu-Han added, "Next time you stand beside me, Jesus, could you push me or something so I know it's you?"

Emma whispered, "I want to come to you, too, so please send me messages."

Then, to their surprise, Jacob spoke. "OK, Jesus, if you really send messages, I want one, too. Amen."

The four friends looked at each other for a moment.

"What do we do, now?" asked Fu-Han. "Just wait for a clue or something?"

Suddenly, Emma jumped to her feet. "I got an idea when we were praying. We got a clubhouse, but we can't decide what kind of club to have. Well, why don't we be God Detectives, and search for all the ways God talks with kids!"

Tabitha looked at Emma. "Wow, that's great," she breathed. "We could talk to all kinds of people and find out what they hear from God."

"That's IF they hear from God," said Jacob.

Emma ignored him. "We could write down all the clues we find in a book!"

Tabitha waved a color pencil in the air. "We could make certificates saying we're God Detectives!"

Fu-Han leapt to his feet. "Then we keep a list on the wall of all the information we find. We cross-reference it on a database and set up a website for future uploads about how people hear from God."

Jacob spoke again. "That's IF they hear from God. If we're going to be real detectives, we have to collect the clues first and make up our minds later."

The others looked at Jacob for a moment. Finally, Emma said, "Jacob's right. We'll get as many clues as we can and then see what the evidence is."

Tabitha opened up her sketchbook. "I think we got *a clue* already."

They stared at her. "Already?"

"Sure," Tabitha replied. "Clue Number One: *God sends messages in different ways, like in stories or like an invisible someone standing beside you.*"

Tabitha began to write the clue in her book. "I'm going to draw a picture for every clue," she said, spreading out her color pencils.

Jacob was quiet and for a moment the others wondered what he was thinking. Then he slapped his thigh. "Well," he said, "we've got our club; we'd better have a sign for the door."

The clubhouse door banged open as the friends burst out. Jacob brought the paint cans so Tabitha could paint the sign. Emma sat on the roof and called out the spelling. Fu-Han hung a green scarf flag beside the door, to make it look official. Then, Jacob nailed the sign to the front of their new headquarters. The four friends looked at it and grinned.

"I guess we're in business," Jacob said. "Watch out, world. Here come the God Detectives!"

Horse Sense

Emma was so excited she could hardly breathe! In a few minutes she would be on a horse, taking her first riding lesson. As she ran to the tall fence that surrounded the riding ring, she saw a bunch of kids already seated on their horses. Emma called out to the only adult in the ring, a man with bright red hair and shiny black boots: "I'm here for the lesson!"

"Sorry – all the horses are taken," shouted the man, not even looking away from his class.

"But I've signed up for this lesson! I want to learn to ride!"

"Class is full," replied the teacher. As if to make it clear that there was no point arguing, he called to his students and told them to ride their horses in a circle around him.

A huge lump formed in Emma's throat and her lip quivered. *There's no horse for me*, she thought. Tears had begun to run down her face. The other students were trotting their horses now. It hurt to watch them, so

Emma turned her back and wandered over to the horse barn.

All the stalls, where the horses rested, seemed empty. However, right at the end of the barn, a flash of gold caught her eye. Curious, Emma walked down the long, dark aisle between the stalls. The golden light gleamed from the last stall on the right. As Emma reached it, the most beautiful horse she had ever seen stuck its head over the gate and blew its sweet, warm breath right on her face.

"Oh, you're wonderful!" Emma whispered.

"You're wonderful, too," said the horse.

For some reason, it seemed quite natural that the horse could talk.

"I wanted to ride, but the class is full," said Emma.

"There is more than one way to ride," replied the horse. "If you're ready, open the gate and we'll be off."

The gate swung open and the lovely creature stepped delicately out of its stall. Although she was a full-sized horse, she was only a little taller than Emma. As the horse moved, her coat glowed – sometimes gold and sometimes white. Her eyes were a deep, chocolate brown.

"But I don't know how to saddle you," said Emma.

"No need," the horse encouraged her. "You can ride without a saddle and hold on to my mane."

The horse's back was warm. Emma wrapped her hands in the long mane and breathed in the scent of the horse: a mixture of sweet alfalfa, clover, and sunlight. Once outside, the horse turned away from the riding ring where the riding lesson was being held and trotted toward the forest.

Emma thought her heart would burst with joy. She was riding! Together they galloped and trotted

through many miles of forest and meadow – sometimes so fast the wind brought tears to her eyes, sometimes so slowly she could see bees buzzing in the flowers. During the whole ride, Emma felt safe. She knew the horse wouldn't put her in danger.

Even so, once she leaned over too far to look at a blue butterfly and slid right off onto the grass! "I thought you would keep me from falling," she said to the horse, rubbing her shoulder with surprise.

The horse's laugh echoed throughout the meadow: "You have to do your part to stay with me, Emma!"

Emma stood on top of a nearby tree stump to climb back onto the horse. They rode for what seemed like hours before Emma caught sight of the horse farm. As they drew closer, she could see the class riding in a circle around their teacher.

"I'm glad there wasn't room for me," she smiled. "This was better."

"There are many different ways to ride," the horse said, for a second time. "And I give each person the kind of ride that is right for them."

"But you're here with me, not there with those other kids," whispered Emma, as she laid her face on the horse's soft neck.

"Oh, I come to them, too," laughed the horse. "I come to every child and to every grownup in the whole world, to help them and to guide them. Some see me and some don't, but I am always close, even to those who *don't* see me."

Emma looked up. As she did, the forest shimmered into pieces of light, like a stained-glass window in the rain. The quiet of the meadow was broken by sounds that swelled loud and soft, ringing in her ears. She looked around in dismay. "What's happening?" she asked.

"Your dream is ending," answered the horse.

"My dream?" she asked. "Is this only a dream? I thought it was real. Must you go…?"

But before she could hear an answer, the light and sounds broke in on the world around her, folding into new colors, which slowly revealed the familiar walls of her own bedroom. It was true; it had been a dream. Instantly, she shut her eyes, trying to bring back the scene of the gentle forest and mysterious horse. But it was no use. They were gone. Emma sat on the edge of her bed, feeling half in one world, half in another.

"If you have a dream from God, you'll know it," said her mother later at breakfast. "You may not remember all of it, but what you *do* remember will seem very wonderful or very important. You'll find yourself thinking of it over and over."

"But, Mom, what do dreams from God mean?" asked Emma.

"Well, it seems to me that dreams can come from God for many reasons. That sure happened to the people in the Bible."

"Like Joseph and his coat of many colors," said Emma.

"That's right," replied Emma's mom. "And God may be saying 'I love you,' or helping you with a problem. Do you think your horse was a message from God?" She stopped stacking dishes to look at Emma.

Emma thought hard. "I don't know. I sure had a loving feeling when I was riding, though."

Her mom smiled and stroked Emma's forehead.

"Will I ever see my horse again?" Emma asked her.

"I guess you can ask God for that," replied her mom. Emma pulled out her God Detectives notebook and walked down the hall to her bedroom. "I don't want to forget this one," she thought, as she sat down on her bed to write: Clue Number Two: *Sometimes God speaks to us in dreams.*

As she gently closed her notebook, a gleam of golden light caught the corner of her eye. She turned quickly and saw in the shimmer of light the faint shape of a horse. For a second, she found herself gazing into two, deep chocolate brown eyes. And then they were gone.

Brother Anton's Tale

Tabitha leaned far, far back on her swing to see the ground racing beneath her. The wind whipped through her braids and the wet smell of autumn earth rose up as she sped by. A second later, she reached the top of the trees, swung her head upright, and gazed into the sky. The familiar flip-flop inside her stomach was scary and made her laugh every single time.

It was playground day for Tabitha and her best friend, Emma. Tabitha's squeals were joined by the sound of four seagulls screeching and flying above them. Emma pointed as they landed next to a man on a nearby park bench. The man was eating his lunch from a brown paper bag and the seagulls thought they were invited.

Tabitha laughed. Then she looked more closely at the man. He was dressed in a long, brown robe, with a rope for a belt. The robe nearly covered the sandals he wore on his feet. Tabitha had never seen anyone like him, except in some pictures of Jesus. Those pictures usually showed Jesus wearing white robes, but maybe he had decided to try a new color.

"Emma, look at that man. Is he Jesus?"

Now it was Emma's turn to laugh. "Jesus! Who? Him?" She pointed her feet to the sky as she took another swing. "I've seen him before. I asked my mom about him. She said he's a… well… um… he's a follower of Saint Francis."

"Who's Saint Francis?" asked Tabitha.

"Mom said he lived a long time ago. She also said that he loved God so much he once preached to the birds."

"I wonder if the man on the bench is getting ready to tell those seagulls about God?" said Tabitha.

"Maybe we should go hear him," Emma suggested. Then, without waiting for Tabitha to reply, she jumped from her swing and began running across the field.

"Wait a minute!" Tabitha called, but it was too late. Emma was headed to the picnic blanket where her mother was feeding baby Brendan.

Just then, Tabitha heard someone call her name. Jacob and Fu-Han skidded to a stop in front of her.

"We ran all the way from your house," Jacob puffed. "Fu-Han figured if you weren't home, you were probably at the park."

Tabitha dragged her runners on the ground mid-swing. "That's good detective work," she said.

"You better believe it," said Fu-Han.

Emma was suddenly with them again. "Hi guys! See that man on the bench over there? Mom says he's a follower of Saint Francis and we're allowed to go talk to him."

"I think he's about to tell those birds about God," added Tabitha. "C'mon!"

The two girls set off at a run. For a second, Jacob and Fu-Han just stood looking at each other, until Fu-Han cried, "Let's go!" Instantly, the two boys sprang into action.

"Who's Saint Francis?!" Jacob called out, as they raced to catch up to the girls. "And why would anyone need to tell the birds about God?" cried Fu-Han. "They already know!"

When the four friends reached the man, he looked up and smiled at them. The seagulls screeched and flew a short distance away.

"Excuse me, sir," said Tabitha. "We're in a club to find out how God talks with people. Are you going to speak to the birds?" She nodded toward Emma. "Her mom said we could talk to you."

The man's smile deepened. Then he folded his lunch bag. Immediately, the seagulls hopped a little closer.

"That sounds like a great club," he said. "I would love to talk to you. My name is Brother Anton and I can tell you a story about how God talked to Saint Francis." He pointed to the grass. "Have a seat with the seagulls."

Brother Anton began. "Saint Francis is also called Francis of Assisi. Many people all around the world love him. But, in his lifetime, he had many struggles. When Francis was a young man, he dreamed about doing mighty things for God. At first, he thought that becoming a knight and fighting in wars would be the best thing to do. So he rode off to war on a beautiful horse, wearing gleaming armor. He was very pleased with himself. But *God* was not pleased and sent him dreams and visions that told him not to hurt others. So Francis turned his horse around. Clearly God did not want him to fight, but what did God want him to do instead? He waited for more dreams and visions, but the message still wasn't clear.

"Francis was sad and confused. One day, he walked through town and out into the countryside. There he found an old, abandoned church called San Damiano. Its walls were crumbling and broken.

"Francis thought to himself, 'Maybe I'll hear God more clearly if I pray in here.'

"Inside, attached to a wall, he found a large colorful crucifix, or cross, with a picture of Jesus painted on it. He knelt and began to speak to God. 'What is your plan for me? I'm confused and I don't know what

to do.' Suddenly, Francis heard a voice! It seemed to be coming from Jesus on the crucifix. The voice said, 'Francis, go now and repair my church, which, as you can see, is in ruins.'

"Here was the message he had been waiting for! And it was so clear! Francis said, 'Thank you, Jesus,' over and over as he began to plan how he would rebuild the broken-down church of San Damiano. Francis didn't know how to build with stone, but that didn't stop him. He collected stones and mixed mortar to hold them in place and the walls grew strong and high."

Fu-Han interrupted: "So God wanted Francis to fix that old church."

"Well, actually," said Brother Anton, "Francis was mistaken! The word 'church' can mean the building Christians worship in, or it can mean all the Christian people. God wasn't asking him to repair the church *building*. God wanted him to repair what some of the Christian leaders were doing. They weren't following

Jesus' teaching about love and kindness and so other people were getting hurt."

"Was God mad at Francis for mixing up the message?" asked Jacob.

"Oh, no," laughed Brother Anton. "God knows we often get messages mixed up. God is happy that we even *try* to understand what the message is. But that's not the end of the story. God opened the hearts of other young men and women so that they would want to *help* Francis. After rebuilding the old church, they all shared the messages that came to them from God, and Francis and his followers learned to understand God's plan much better."

Emma stared at him. "Why couldn't God have explained more clearly right from the start?"

Brother Anton sighed. "I don't know, my dear. Sometimes we get messages from God mixed up because we think we already know what they mean. Asking God questions about the message can help. Also, sometimes when you are trying to understand God's messages it can be like doing a jigsaw puzzle. For a while, the puzzle doesn't look like anything. And then, all of a sudden – even though it's not finished – you see the picture!"

"I got a puzzle for my birthday last summer," sighed Jacob. "It *still* isn't finished!"

Brother Anton chuckled. "Yes, indeed. Sometimes, it can take a long time before the message starts to make sense. Thank goodness God sends us messages all the time, so there are always some that we can understand right away. For example, Francis knew that God is always sending us the message 'I love you.' We can see that message in this wonderful world of plants and animals and rocks and water and air and people. Why, all of creation is an incredible gift that shows how much God loves us!"

Tabitha smoothed the grass in front of her. "I wish I had been there to hear Jesus talk to Francis."

"Yes, so do I," replied Brother Anton. "On the other hand, if we had been there, we might not have heard anything. God often speaks quietly into our hearts. Some say it's like a voice; others say a message just comes into their heads and they know what to do. In any case, we know it's a message from God because it comes with a feeling of love. *God would never tell you to do anything to harm yourself or another being.*"

Just then, they heard Emma's mom call. "Time to pack up, kids! It's going to be suppertime soon."

"Coming!" Emma called back.

The four God Detectives picked themselves up from the grass and Tabitha turned to Brother Anton. "Thanks for telling us about Francis. We've got Clue Number Three."

"And what is that?" he asked.

Fu-Han read what he had already written: *God sends us lots of messages and it's okay if it takes a long time to figure them out.*

Brother Anton smiled. As the four friends ran back across the field, all the seagulls rose into the air as one, circling and calling to the sky.

Clue Number 3
God sends us messages and it's okay if it takes us a long time to figure them out.

The Two Voices

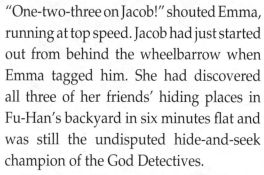

"One-two-three on Jacob!" shouted Emma, running at top speed. Jacob had just started out from behind the wheelbarrow when Emma tagged him. She had discovered all three of her friends' hiding places in Fu-Han's backyard in six minutes flat and was still the undisputed hide-and-seek champion of the God Detectives.

"I'm thirsty!" Jacob said breathlessly, dropping to the floor inside the clubhouse with the others. "Getting defeated by Emma takes a lot out of a kid."

Tabitha, who was already lying down, nodded in agreement.

"I'll go get us some drinks," said Fu-Han, standing up to brush the dirt off his clothes from when he had crawled on his belly through the bushes.

The kitchen was cool and dark and filled with the sweet smell of fresh baking. As Fu-Han poured four cups of water, he noticed a plate on the counter, piled high with cookies. Chocolate chip, his favorite! Fu-Han could almost taste them.

As he looked at the cookies, Fu-Han heard a little voice inside him: "Those cookies would taste soooo good. And there are so many, your parents wouldn't notice if you took one. And even if they *did* notice, they would probably be glad, because they wouldn't want you to be hungry. Why don't you eat one?"

That's a good idea, thought Fu-Han, and he walked towards the plate. Just as he reached out his hand to take a big cookie chock full of chocolate chips, another little voice spoke inside of him.

"Sure you're hungry. Sure your parents might give you a cookie if you ask. But if you just take that cookie, it's stealing."

Fu-Han pulled his hand back and thought a bit.

"Well, yes, it would be stealing," soothed the first voice, "but it wouldn't really hurt anyone if you took a cookie; there are so many. And if they didn't know you did it, who could be upset?"

Fu-Han's hand moved toward the cookies again.

"Wait a minute, buddy," said the second voice. "How would *you* feel if a friend took something of yours without asking?"

Fu-Han considered for a moment. *I guess I wouldn't really trust that friend anymore*, he thought back.

"But no one will know," said the first voice.

Fu-Han turned away from the cookies. "But *I* would know," he said out loud. "And I wouldn't feel very good, because I want my friends to trust me."

Just then, Fu-Han's mom and dad walked into the kitchen. "Hey, you saw we baked your favorite cookies," said his dad.

"Why don't you call everyone in from outside? It's time for a snack," his mom encouraged.

Fu-Han was so relieved, he ran back to the clubhouse.

By the time he reached the door, he had decided to tell the other club members about the two voices. "I've heard those voices before, but I never really thought about them. Do you ever hear voices?"

"Yeah, I do," Emma answered. "Sometimes they speak words and other times I just kind of know what they're saying. What do you think they are?"

Fu-Han considered. "Well, one seems to be a bad voice and one is a good voice."

Tabitha said, "I know the good voice is our conscience. I don't know what the bad voice is."

Jacob held up one of the action figures he always carried in his pocket. It had a scowl on its face and held a huge sword in its two hands. In his scary voice, he whispered, "Maybe the bad voice is The Dark Lord. Maybe the voices are a fight between good and evil. Which side will win, I wonder."

The friends became silent and looked at each other uneasily.

"Hey!" called a voice suddenly, causing them all to jump. "I never met kids who didn't like cookies!" It was Fu-Han's dad. "You'd better get in here while there are still some left!"

The club members grinned in relief.

"Race you," yelled Emma, and they all ran to the house.

These cookies taste as good as the voice said they would, Fu-Han thought, as they sat in the kitchen enjoying the snack together.

Just at that moment, his dad said, "Well, a little voice is telling me to take another cookie, but I think two is enough."

Fu-Han turned to him. "Do you have different voices inside you?"

"Of course," said Fu-Han's dad. "Everyone does."

"We were wondering if one voice is our conscience..." said Tabitha.

"... and the other voice is an evil force!" added Jacob.

"Goodness, no!" replied Fu-Han's dad. "There's no evil inside you. That voice is what adults call our ego, or our small self. The other voice is our conscience, or big self. The ego isn't evil or bad. God wouldn't put something bad inside us. The ego just isn't as wise as the conscience."

"But it tells us to do bad things," said Fu-Han.

Fu-Han's mom walked across the room to a small painting of a mountain lake that was drying on an easel. She was an artist. "Look at this little picture," she said. "Your ego sees the little picture of a situation. It tries to help you, but often, it doesn't think of how your actions will affect other people. So if you ignore your conscience and only listen to your ego, you might do something that suits you just fine, but that hurts others."

She swung her arm around to show the whole world. "Your conscience sees the bigger picture. It wants to help both you and others. Now, *God* sees the biggest picture of all and is always thinking of *everyone*. God gives messages and suggestions to both the ego and the conscience, but the conscience hears more clearly."

Emma was the first to speak. "So should we plug our ears when we hear our ego?"

Fu-Han's dad answered. "No, don't ignore your ego, Emma. Treat it gently, like the way you treat your baby brother. What do you do when he does something he shouldn't? Do you hit him?"

"No, we just stop him and tell him the right thing to do," said Emma.

"Right," said Fu-Han's dad. "It's the same with your ego. Be gentle and firm with your ego and explain the bigger picture to it."

Fu-Han looked relieved. "Wow, I'm glad I don't have something bad inside me."

His dad continued: "Remember how we always tell you to trust your feelings and to go away if an adult or child does something that doesn't feel right to you? And to tell an adult you trust about anything else that scares you?"

The kids nodded.

"As well as talking to an adult, you can also talk to Jesus when something upsets you," his dad finished.

The kids nodded again as Fu-Han's dad stood up.

"Now, you kids get busy and finish off those

cookies," he said with a smile, as he went back to his computer.

Fu-Han pulled his God Detective notebook out of his pocket. "Okay, that's Clue Number Four," he said to his friends: *"God speaks to our ego and to our conscience, but our conscience understands God better."*

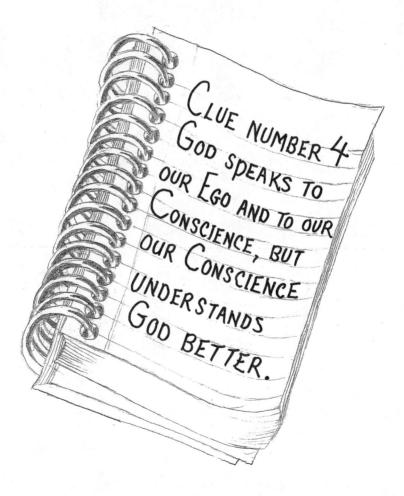

Mr. Sparkles

"Emma, have you finished packing?" called her mom. "Tabitha is here."

It was Saturday morning and Emma had been waiting for Tabitha to pick her up for a swim date and sleepover. She raced down the stairs with her backpack swinging.

"See ya later!" she said, hugging her mom goodbye. Then she ran to the car. When she and Tabitha both said "Hi" at the exact same moment, they burst out laughing.

Tabitha's mother spoke to her from the driver's seat: "Good to see you, Emma. Just slide in beside Amy."

Tabitha was sitting up front with her mom, while her five-year-old sister, Amy, was in the back. Emma opened the door and started to get in when Amy said, "Careful, Emma, don't sit on Mr. Sparkles."

Emma looked at the empty seat. "I don't see anyone there."

"I'm the only one that can see him," explained Amy.

Emma was puzzled. "Then how will I know where he is?" she asked.

"I'll tell you," Amy replied. "Just sit close to the door and you won't squish him."

Emma thought this was pretty weird, but she did as she was told.

Later, at lunch, Emma was about to sit in a chair that was already pulled out from the table, when Amy commanded, "Don't sit there! That's Mr. Sparkles' chair!"

Everyone else acted like it was normal to have an invisible guest at the lunch table, so Emma didn't say anything. During the meal, Amy sometimes looked over at the empty chair and said something, or seemed to be answering a question.

Really weird, thought Emma.

After lunch, Emma and Tabitha went into Tabitha's room to get their towels and swimsuits. Emma was bursting to ask about Mr. Sparkles.

"Well, Amy says he's a dolphin that talks," Tabitha explained. "He's so little you can hold him in one hand. And he's rainbow-colored."

"Where did he come from?" asked Emma.

Tabitha shoved her bathing suit into a bag, along with her towel. "We don't know. Last year, when Amy was four, she fell at preschool and cut her lip open.

The teachers couldn't find Mom or Dad, so they took Amy to the hospital to get stitched up. Amy wouldn't stop crying and fighting the doctor. Then, the nurse said a weird thing happened. Amy just stopped crying. She looked like she was listening to something and she calmed right down. Later, when Dad asked her what happened, Amy said that Mr. Sparkles had come and had hummed to her to make her feel better. And he's been with her ever since."

"But he's not *real*," said Emma. "Why don't you tell her?"

"Dad says lots of kids have imaginary friends that play with them or help them," Tabitha explained.

Emma swung her backpack onto her shoulders. "Well, I've never had an imaginary friend!"

"Nope, me neither," replied Tabitha, as she zipped up her swim-bag and started for the door.

Later, as the three girls were changing at the swimming pool, Emma watched Amy chat with Mr. Sparkles. She still thought it was weird and wondered if it would be better to tell Amy that Mr. Sparkles wasn't real.

As the girls walked out of the shower room and onto the pool deck, Amy pointed excitedly at a pile of pool toys at the far end of the pool. Lifeguards were handing them out to a group of kids. "I want one!" Amy cried, and broke into a run on the slippery surface.

"Amy, no!" Tabitha's voice was swallowed up by the sound of playful screams and splashing.

Tabitha shouted again, but Amy continued to run at full speed towards the toys. Then, all of a sudden, she stopped. When the older girls caught up with her, she said to them, "Mr. Sparkles told me not to run. I could slip and hurt myself. I knew that, but I forgot."

Emma felt like she had heard just about enough of Mr. Sparkles and was just about to say so, when Amy tilted her head as if she were listening. Then she looked straight at Emma. "Mr. Sparkles says he's happy to see your horse."

"My horse!" exclaimed Emma, startled. "What are you talking about? I don't have a horse."

"I can't see her," said Amy, "but Mr. Sparkles can."

In an instant, the roar of the pool room faded to a dull, far-away echo. Emma felt sunlight on her skin and breathed in the scent of sweet hay and clover. Her heart began to race. Standing just behind her, she felt the horse from her dream! In her mind, she saw the horse dip its beautiful head towards her.

"I give everyone what they need," it breathed. "Amy needs Mr. Sparkles."

"So Mr. Sparkles is real," murmured Emma to the beautiful creature.

Tabitha glanced at her with a puzzled look.

"Mr. Sparkles says sometimes the Spirit sends messengers," said Amy. "That doesn't make sense. I want to go swimming."

Emma stared at the place, where, in her mind, she had seen the horse just a moment ago. *I'll have to remember to write it down when I get home*, she thought. Clue Number Five: *God can use imaginary friends to send us messages.*

6

The Sign

Fu-Han pulled on the blue and green striped pants and knew right away they were too big.

"Here," said Albert's auntie, walking over with safety pins. "No one will see these once you put your tunic on." She handed him the shimmery purple shirt.

Fu-Han was playing one of the magi in the church's Christmas pageant. It was his job to walk up the aisle with two other magi, and give his box of gold to Baby Jesus, while the people sang *We Three Kings*.

Tomorrow would be Christmas Eve. Lots of people would come to watch the story of Jesus' birth. Jacob and Albert were the other magi. Once they were dressed, they sat on a bench away from the commotion and watched the other kids trying on costumes. Albert's auntie was using her safety pins a lot.

"Do we go in when they start singing?" Jacob asked Albert and Fu-Han.

"Nope," said Albert. "We wait until they sing, *'following yonder star.'* When the spotlight shines on the star over the stable, then we start walking." Jacob nodded, setting his frankincense on his lap.

Fu-Han's brow furrowed. "Why would the magi follow a star anyway?" he asked. "Why would they think a star meant anything?"

"I don't know," replied Albert. "Maybe it's a sign. Our elders say all the time that the Creator uses signs to speak to us."

Fu-Han was thoughtful. "Another way God gives us messages," he murmured.

Suddenly it was quiet in the room. All the angels, shepherds, and animals had left to practice their scenes. Albert's auntie pulled up a chair and sat down beside them with a sigh. "Well, that's done! Everyone has a costume."

"Auntie Vivian, I'm telling Jacob and Fu-Han about signs from the Creator, like the star the magi followed. Tell them the story of your eagle."

"All right, kids; we probably have a few minutes until they want you on stage," said his aunt. "I'll tell you about my eagle."

She sat for a moment, staring out over their heads. "A few months ago, I was trying to decide whether to stay in the house I have now, or find a new home. It was confusing. One day I would think I should stay where I was; the next day, I would decide the new home was better. I wondered which place the Creator wanted me to live in, because the Great Spirit sends us messages telling us which choice will be best for us.

"So I went down to the beach, by the ocean, to pray. I pray there many times because I often hear God's messages more clearly when I am surrounded by nature. This time was very different, right from the start. I sat on a log close to the water and began to pray: 'Great Spirit, would it be better for me to stay where I am, or should I move?' As I prayed, I watched and felt and heard and smelled all the nature around me. The sun was warm on my skin, the breeze smelled of

seaweed and salt, the sand was cool and rough under my feet, and the waves were changing from blue to green to gray.

"There was a large eagle sitting on the branch of a tall fir tree. His white head gleamed as he turned and looked at me. I was surprised to see this eagle at the beach. I expected it to fly away when it saw me, but I was surprised again, because it stayed with me for more than an hour. This is strange for an eagle to do. Usually it would be off fishing. But I was very glad the eagle was there. We were the first people to live in this land, and right from the early days we knew that the eagle was a powerful sign from God, for our people. But it can mean many things and I knew I would have to wait until God put the meaning into my mind and heart.

"As we sat together, I thought of the eagle and how solidly it was sitting on its branch. Staying in its place. As I prayed, I thought about my two possible homes. I started to wonder if the best thing for me to do right now was to stay in my place – like the eagle. Was this what God was saying to me? That idea felt right to me and I was peaceful when I thought about the home I already had. So I decided God wanted me to stay in my place and I gave thanks to the Great Spirit for this message."

Fu-Han asked, "If I saw an eagle, would it be a sign for me?"

"Maybe. Maybe not," said Auntie Vivian. "The eagle by itself is not a sign. But God can use it to send us a message if God wants to. You know, the Star of Bethlehem was not a sign all by itself, either. Many people saw that star, but only the magi knew it was a sign. That's because the magi had opened their hearts and minds to notice a message from God in it. That same star didn't mean anything to the shepherds, so God sent angels to them to give the news of Jesus' birth. Our Creator uses many different ways to send people messages. The Great Spirit gave me the idea to go to the beach, just as the eagle was there. Then, because I was willing to receive God's message, the eagle became a sign for me."

Jacob said, "So, *God sends us messages in nature.*"

Fu-Han whispered, "Clue Number Six."

"That's right," replied Auntie Vivian. She rose to her feet and slipped the safety pins into her pocket. "If we watch and listen, there will be a sign for each one of us."

Clue #6
God sends
us messages
in nature.

What Can a Kid Do?

"Happy New Year!" Emma swung the front door wide open even before the doorbell rang. Tabitha beamed at her from the front steps, her little sister, Amy, by her side, and her parents behind her.

"You mean New Year's *Eve*..." said Jacob, joining them at the door. "New Year's Day is tomorrow."

Tabitha shook her long winter coat from her shoulders and let her parents pile their own into her arms until she could hardly be seen. "Help!" she cried. "I'm being smothered by a winter coat monster!"

Emma laughed and steered the moving pile into the bedroom.

The doorbell rang again. This time it was Fu-Han and his parents. Jacob and Fu-Han quickly disappeared to compare action figure Christmas presents.

When Emma's mom put on some ABBA music, everybody knew the party had really begun. When they weren't dancing, the grownups and kids took turns playing their favorite songs for each other, Tabitha took pictures of everybody when they weren't watching, and Baby Brendan played peek-a-boo under the table until he fell asleep there.

Fu-Han's mother passed around a tray of dried fruits, sweets, and candies. She explained that it was called the Tray of Togetherness, or *Chuen-hop* in Chinese. "This is one way Chinese people welcome guests and relatives during our New Year. Even though the Chinese New Year is over a month away, I thought it would be good to bring the Tray of Togetherness to this Western New Year's party."

Later that evening, Jacob into the living room with a bowl of popcorn and was surprised to hear the grownups talking about war. Fu-Han's dad was holding a carrot stick in his hand, but forgetting to eat it. "I heard on the news that some of the fighters were as young as 12," he was saying. "War is terrible no matter who is fighting, but to think of children being taught to kill…"

Jacob's mom added, "So much for the peace agreement. Now there's more fighting."

Jacob could hear Fu-Han, Tabitha, and Emma laughing in the other room, but in this room there was no laughter. Jacob had been happy, but now he suddenly felt sad. The sadness inside him was like a pain. *How can I enjoy this party when there are wars happening?* he thought. *Kids all over the world are being injured and killed, or even killing other people.*

No one noticed Jacob leave the room. He felt like being alone, so he wandered into the den. It was dark, except in one corner where five candles shaped like stars floated in a crystal bowl filled with water. He sat on a chair and watched the flickering candlelight. *It's beautiful*, he thought, *but it doesn't make the pain go away.*

The dark slowly closed in around him as he sat thinking. The wavering shadows seemed to say "You're alone, you're alone…" In that dark place, a voice rose up inside him and, to his surprise, it was his own: "Jesus, what do I do to feel better?"

As soon as he had spoken, however, Jacob felt even more pain! It was strange, because he noticed the pain inside him, but it didn't seem to be his own. It was a different and much larger Pain and Sadness. His own sadness seemed like a small ant compared to this other one. This Sadness was like an elephant – no, like a planet – no, even bigger. *It's so big, it could swallow me up*, worried Jacob.

Then, as he thought about this, the huge Sadness and Pain seemed to move toward him. It moved like the wave that had once knocked him over at the beach! As the Pain touched him, Jacob seemed to be dragged into its undertow. *Oh, no!* he thought. *I'm going to drown in sadness! What's happening to me?*

What actually happened was the last thing he would ever have expected. Inside the larger Pain, Jacob discovered something even stronger – Love. A great, huge blanket of Love. Every part of him tingled with it. Rising up inside him like a wave, Jacob felt a happiness he had never felt before. His pain and sadness were still there and the gigantic Pain was still there. Yet he felt the immense Love protecting him at the same time.

As Jacob rested in the Love, he realized that it was bigger than forever. It had no end. It was infinite. Part of him was scared, because it was so big, and part of him wanted to stay there until the end of time. The Love seemed to have become part of every cell in his body. *What's happening?* he wondered again.

And then he wasn't alone, although no one had come into the room. Something had changed. There was an invisible "someone" standing beside him.

Hi, Jacob said in his mind to the invisible someone. An answer came, but not in words. Jacob felt another surge of love and delight instead. The invisible someone was sending him Love! It was hard for Jacob even to think. The wave of Love was so strong it seemed to take his thoughts away.

Finally, he thought back, *Who are you?*

I'm Jesus, came the answer. *I'm so happy you are with me.*

For a long time, Jacob just floated, feeling happy and loved. After a while, though, he noticed that he couldn't feel Jesus anymore.

Jacob looked around the room. One candle in the bowl had burned out. He had been there for a long time! Just then, Emma came into the room followed by Tabitha and Fu-Han. "Mom and I turned this room into a quiet space on purpose," Emma was explaining to the others.

Jacob looked up and the love that was still inside him seemed to flow out of his body toward his friends. He felt so much love for everyone and everything that he thought his heart would burst.

"Hey, Jake, I didn't know you were in here," said Fu-Han. He was about to say something else, but he suddenly stopped himself. Yes.

Tabitha squinted. "Hey, what's up, Jacob? You look different. Kind of glowy."

Jacob didn't know what to say, so he just smiled back at them. Then he whispered, "Jesus loves us so much. I was feeling sad and he came to help me."

"He did?" asked Tabitha. "What did he look like?"

Jacob shook his head. "I can't remember what he looked like, but I remember what he did. I was feeling really bad about the wars in the world. I'm still really hurting about it, but now it feels like there's a blanket of love around the pain. I want Jesus to come like this whenever I'm sad."

Fu-Han raised his eyebrows and smiled. "Hey, do you know what you're saying?" he asked. "Jesus came to you and gave you a message!"

Jacob looked up. "You're right; he did! Wow!" He looked at his friends. "Why didn't you tell me it feels like this when Jesus sends you a message?"

Emma's eyes bugged out. "It doesn't! Or... well... it didn't for me. When I got a message from God, my dream horse brought it to me."

"Jesus talked to me in a Bible story," Tabitha said. Then she added, "But my sister, Amy, says her imaginary friend gives her help from God."

Fu-Han sat down beside Jacob. "Plus, there's Alfred's Aunt Vivian. She says she noticed God's message in an eagle."

Emma interrupted excitedly. "And Fu-Han, you heard two voices in your head and had to figure out which one understood God better!"

"I'm so confused," said Jacob. "Why doesn't God talk to us in just one way so that we always know who it is?"

Tabitha smiled and shook her head, making the beads on her cornrows tinkle like tiny bells. *"Remember,"* she said, *"God gives every person just what they need."*

"I wish everyone could feel God like this," said Jacob. "If they did, I know there wouldn't be any more wars." He let out a sad sigh. "But what can a kid do to bring peace, anyway? What can we do?"

The four friends sat staring into the crystal bowl and the remaining candlelight.

Tabitha broke the silence cautiously. "Brother Anton said that Saint Francis didn't start out being very good at getting God's messages. But he kept on asking God, 'What next?' That's what I'm going to do."

"Being a God Detective helps," Emma added. "Mom says she's noticed a difference in me since I became one. She said I don't get bugged so much by Baby Brendan and I'm more patient with him. She said that all three of us are happier in the house because of that."

Fu-Han pulled his God Detectives notebook from his pocket and scanned what he had written. "I think it's possible," he said thoughtfully, "that praying makes the world a more peaceful place, even before you get up to do something about it."

"What makes you say that?" asked Jacob.

"I don't know yet, really," Fu-Han replied. "It just seems like the people we've talked to act more peaceful and they make me feel more peaceful, too. I'll have to do more research on that one."

"Dad says that some people talk so much to God they don't leave room for God to talk to *them*," said Jacob.

"All this has got to be another clue," declared Tabitha with satisfaction. *"God sends us messages of love, so we can share love with the world too."*

"Clue Number Seven," said Fu-Han, snapping his notebook shut.

"Hey, you guys!" cried Emma. "While you were talking, I got an idea! Let's keep on being God Detectives this whole new year and see if the world changes!"

Tabitha grinned. "I was hoping you'd say that. I know three people I want to talk to already."

"We could contact other God Detectives, if there are any, anywhere..." suggested Emma.

"We can have a secret handshake and all get cell phones!" added Fu-Han.

Suddenly, Jacob stopped them. "Listen," he said, gesturing for silence. "It's here!"

For a second, the four friends looked at him, confused. Then they followed his gaze past the shimmering bowl to the clock on the mantel. The big hand had just moved to midnight. From the other room came the sound of the grownups loudly singing the New Year's song.

"Oh, man, do they ever need our help," groaned Emma. Then she smiled. "Happy New Year, God Detectives!"

Clue #7

God sends us
messages of love
so we can
share love with
the world too.

Do You Want to Become a God Detective?

Visit the God Detectives on their website!

Tell us *your* stories, print off drawings and a certificate to color, download songs, read about the four friends, and learn more about the grownups who wrote the book at:

www.goddetectives.com

Use the following pages to keep your own notes or write your own stories about how God talks to you.

Visit www.goddetectives.com, where you can type in your own story. It may be posted on the website.

Notes for Adults

Sharing our spiritual experiences with children

Talking to children about experiences of God we had when we ourselves were children, or even after we became adults, may help them in many ways. They may begin to realize, for example, that divine/human interaction is normal and common. They may begin to understand that God relates to us in many different ways. Talking to children about our spiritual experiences can also give them spiritual language. And sharing important experiences of any kind may develop stronger bonds between the adults and children involved.

Telling children about our spiritual experiences can also be *unhelpful*. Children may judge our experience as more important than their own. Or they may stop their sharing and politely switch from speaking to listening. Here are some tips for sharing our own "God touches," intended to affirm and support the child's experiences.

1. Prior to talking with a child, spend some time remembering your own childhood spiritual experiences. How were your heart and mind stirred by the divine? Write those experiences down or talk to an adult first. Many adults rarely, if ever, speak about their spiritual experiences. The first few times may feel awkward. If you can't remember any spiritual experiences, bring to prayer your desire to hear and see how God has been present in your life. Doing this may help memories to surface.

2. Sharing our experiences always takes the conversational "ball" away from the child. After you tell your story, give the ball back, by saying something like, "So that's what happened when I was

six. Can you tell me more about what happened to you?" If you just fall silent after telling your story, the child may not realize it is now their turn to talk.

3. Keep your sharing short, or kids may lose interest or be overloaded with information.

4. Never say, "The same thing happened to me." Your story will always have similarities and differences to the child's. Be more tentative: "I'll tell you a story about something that happened to me, which may be a bit like your experience." Let the child make his or her own connections.

5. Sharing our experiences is more helpful when those experiences are on a similar "level" to the child's story. If the child speaks of feeling "one with the whole world" and you have never had this feeling, it is enough to listen respectfully instead of sharing a different type of spiritual experience of your own. Similarly, children may feel diminished if you respond to their small divine touches with a mind-blowing dream of angels taking you to the throne of God.

1. Let the Children Come to Me

 Children already experience God before an adult first speaks to them about things spiritual. We recognize that children are spiritual beings and we want to help them value their spiritual nature so that it can become deeper and sustain them all through their lives. We can best assist children's spiritual growth by acknowledging, honoring, affirming, and giving words for the child-God relationship that is already developing within them. In other words, we are to be spiritual directors or accompaniers rather than faith educators; gardeners nurturing spirituality rather than architects designing children's faith. (Ralph Mattson and Thom Black, *Discovering Your Child's Design*, Elgin, IL: David C. Cook Publishing Co., 1992)

C. S. Lewis, author of the children's books about the mythical land of Narnia and the Christ figure, Aslan, describes "a particular recurrent experience which dominated my childhood and adolescence." It is one he believes is shared by children and adults, but is often misunderstood. "The experience is one of intense longing. It is distinguished from other longings by two things. In the first place, though the sense of want is acute and even painful, yet the mere wanting is felt to be somehow a delight… In the second place, there is a special mystery about the object of this Desire." People often mistake whatever they are focusing on at the time for the object of desire. The true object of this longing is God.

Tabitha's parents nurtured her faith by reading her the Bible story about Jesus and the children. Because of their own love for the Bible and because they were able to share it, she was "drawn in." Tabitha found herself *living*, rather than just *listening to*, the familiar tale. This experience aroused in her a longing for a relationship with Jesus. Her excitement about her experience aroused the longing of her three friends. And the God Detectives were born.

Questions to consider with children

1. Have you ever felt as if you were part of a story like Tabitha did?
2. If you could tell Jesus (or God) anything, what would it be?
3. Do you have a favorite Bible story? If so, what is it and what makes it your favorite?

2. Horse Sense

Do you ever wonder what we dream about in the womb? Dreams are the inner conversations of the soul. They comfort, sort through struggles, bring issues to the surface, remind us of forgotten things, lift our lives into bold relief. Dreams are a powerful means by which God can give us intuitions and nudgings.

Psychologically, dreams are significant. A great amount of research is currently being done on dreaming and sleeping. Researchers are finding that sleep significantly helps us reorganize memories and solve problems. Numerous insights in the world of medicine, science, and art came after "sleeping on a problem."

In the Bible, dreams are considered of great importance. Joseph (of the many-colored coat) has dreams that warn of an impending drought. On two occasions, the other important Joseph (husband of Mary) is given direction in dreams: the first time, that he should proceed with his marriage commitment to Mary even though she is pregnant; the second time, that he should flee with his young family to Egypt to avoid the wrath of King Herod. In all of this, we see God guiding, supporting, and teaching.

In this story, Emma meets a Christ- or God-figure in the form of a horse. She learns that God comes to each person in a different way. God offers love, support, and guidance in the manner that is right for each person.

It could be that in our dreams we are most receptive to the voice of the Spirit. The trouble is, not every dream is sent by God. Not all messages from God are clear at first; sometimes we only know in retrospect that we were being guided by forces beyond us. And often it is in combination with other incidents, coincidences, and intuitive leadings that we discern that we are being given direction. We need to respect the importance of each child's dream, neither telling them what it was about or dismissing the possibility that it might hold wisdom. If children are used to hearing and speaking about dreams, they will be more receptive to the divinely inspired ones.

Some adults show interest only if a child has a nightmare or other disturbing dream. Positive dreams are more likely to be ignored. We can show children that we value all dreams by routinely asking, "Did anyone dream last night?" at the breakfast table. It may be tempting to try to analyze the child's dream, but it is probably not helpful. If there is a meaning for the dreamer, it will continue to "work" in him or her until it surfaces. If a child asks what you think it means, it might be better to redirect the question back to the child: "It's your dream; what does it say to you?"

Children may find it useful to keep a dream journal. This might be part of a God Detectives booklet, if you choose to make one. If dreams are recorded through drawing or writing, the dreamer will become familiar over time with their own rhythms and symbols, and may become better able to discern the nudgings of God in their lives.

Questions to consider with children

1. Have you ever had a dream that reminded you of something you had forgotten?
2. Have you ever had a dream that solved a problem? Or that you didn't understand at all?
3. What did the Horse do and say in Emma's dream?
4. Why didn't the Horse keep Emma from falling off when she leaned over too far?

3. Brother Anton's Tale

Christians are sometimes referred to as "people of the Book" (the "book" being the Bible). We love to hear a good story and to tell a good story. Much of our Christian wisdom comes from our sharing the tales of women and men in the Bible, the history of Christianity, and the stories of our own faith and experiences.

When these stories are told as examples of how God speaks to us, they can encourage children to look for God's messages in their own daily lives. Sometimes, though, adults tell these stories to children to put certain Christians on a kind of pedestal – to show how different they are from us. When this meaning is given, children are more likely to dismiss or ignore their own God touches. They will not look for God in their lives.

A woman once told this story at a workshop on spiritual discernment: "I've been a Catholic nun since I was 18. I had just entered the convent when a priest asked about my prayer life. I said that ever since I had been a very young child I had occasionally heard Jesus speak to me. The priest replied that Jesus wouldn't speak to me; I wasn't spiritually evolved enough. I was crushed, but I thought he must be right. Even though they continued, I never told anyone else about my conversations with Jesus. Now, in my 80s, I realize how much spiritual closeness I have missed with my sisters."

Questions to consider with children

1. Have you ever met a grownup who taught you something about God? Who was this and what did they say?

2. Have you ever received a message from God like Saint Francis did?

3. Brother Anton said God is always sending us the message "I love you," by giving us such a beautiful world. How do you show someone you love them without words?

4. The Two Voices

Nancy tells this story: "I was giving a workshop for adults on spiritual discernment in Louisville, Kentucky. One of the participants, Sr. Mary Cabrini Hatley, OSU, taught religion at the nearby Ursuline Montessori Elementary School. She asked if I would meet her students and tell them a story. The next day I was seated with the class of 25 six- to eight-year-olds. The children represented a number of Christian denominations, as well as some other faith traditions. I told them the story of the cookies and the two voices. When I asked if they heard voices like that inside them, there was a chorus of "Yeses" and many of the children started giving me examples. "What would you call those voices?" I asked. One girl said, "The first is the voice of my selfishness and the second is my conscience." A boy immediately "corrected" her: "No, the first voice is the Devil." Many of the children nodded nervously. Sr. Cabrini looked horrified and exclaimed, "I didn't teach them that!"

At this young age, children often think in polar opposite terms. They tend to judge people and experiences as wholly good or wholly bad. Popular books and movies are based on this simple dichotomy. The movie *The Chronicles of Narnia* is portrayed in reviews as a struggle between the Christ-figure Aslan, the lion, and the evil white witch. J. K. Rowling, author of the *Harry Potter* series of books, describes the character Voldemort as "the most evil Wizard for hundreds and hundreds of years." *Star Wars'* Darth Vader is referred to as "The Dark Lord." Sauron of *Lord of the Rings* is described as the "embodiment of Evil."

If children think their ego is bad, they may distrust themselves, deny they have this inner voice, and/or try to repress or do away with this part of themselves. *The Two Voices* tells them clearly that their ego is not bad or evil. Instead, the story describes us, as human beings, constantly growing toward our Maker, whose vision of the "big picture" we wish to develop. This way of describing ourselves models forgiveness, so that we can be freed to grow. Blaming, fearing, or projecting all evil onto one person or onto one part of ourselves has never resulted in the transformation God wants to work out within us.

With the proliferation of books and movies that portray a fight between "good" and "evil," it is very important for Christians to clarify their own beliefs about this topic. The prayer Jesus taught us – the Lord's Prayer – is said daily by adults and children around the world and includes the phrase "deliver us from evil." Children wonder about this statement, which they hear and say so often. Christians vary widely in their beliefs about the nature of evil; some think of it as an entity called Satan or the Devil, others as an energy field created by centuries of human cruelty. By clarifying your own beliefs, you will be ready when your children question you about Jesus' prayer.

Questions to consider with children

1. Have you ever heard the two kinds of voices that Fu-Han did?
2. What helped you decide what you were going to do?
3. Who do you talk to when you need to make a decision?

5. Mr. Sparkles

Current research suggests that 65 percent of children up to age seven may have imaginary companions. The imaginary companions can range from a 200-year-old man who comes into the child's life "whenever I have problems and want someone wise to talk to," to a pocket-sized purple elephant who makes the child laugh with silly jokes. The vast majority of imaginary companions function in the following ways. They

- love the child unconditionally
- identify and encourage the child's good qualities
- comfort the child when he or she is scared or in pain
- answer questions about life and death
- serve as a playmate and companion, particularly when the child is lonely.

Research shows that children with imaginary companions are very similar to children without them. The three main differences are that children with imaginary companions

- learn to see other people's point of view, and develop empathy at an earlier age
- are able to sit still and focus their attention for longer periods of time
- tend to watch significantly less television because their fantasy world is so entertaining.

All of these qualities greatly benefit the child's spiritual formation. Studies show that older children, adolescents, and even some adults have imaginary companions. Because our society does not generally support imaginary companions after the preschool years, older children and adults rarely talk about their imaginary friends.

With such loving, life-giving functions, God is obviously present in these experiences. But how? Does the Holy Spirit become a rainbow-colored dolphin for Amy? Is the 200-year-old man a guardian angel? Does God create the imaginary companion to meet the child's need? We can't know for certain. Yet we do know that imaginary companions can help our children develop spiritual gifts and self-esteem.

What can the adult do?

- Acknowledge the imaginary companion without trying to change it or to enter into direct contact without the child's permission.
- Show gratitude for all the ways God talks with us, including through imaginary friends.
- Don't worry if the imaginary companion stays into adolescence. It is a psychologically healthy thing.
- Don't worry if your child does not have an imaginary companion.

In a very few cases, imaginary companions are negative, blaming, or tell kids to do hurtful things. Adults can help by doing the same kinds of things they would do when children are concerned about "the monster" in the closet or under the bed.

- Ask God to change the imaginary companion's heart to be more loving.
- Ask God for another companion to deal with the first. Ask the child what kind of new companion they think God will send.
- Encourage the child to draw the negative companion and then draw it again with changes that will help it be happy and peaceful (for example, by changing its appearance or size). A good resource is Marjorie Taylor's *Imaginary Companions and the Children Who Create Them* (NY: Oxford University Press, 1999).

Questions to consider with children

1. Is Mr. Sparkles a good friend?
2. Have you ever had an imaginary companion?
3. Do you think an imaginary friend might say something that God might want you to know?

6. The Sign

Nancy relates, "Over the years, Linnea and I have heard many people share stories about signs from God. We decided that we didn't want to "make up" a sign when there were so many great stories about real leadings from God to draw upon. But whose story to use? Christians of aboriginal descent are particularly sensitive to signs. I hoped I would find such a person who would tell me a true story that might be edited to fit within the needs of our book.

February 2005 found me at Vancouver School of Theology, ready to be theme presenter for the "Children and the Church Conference." I was sitting alone in the nearly empty cafeteria the night before the conference. A First Nations woman who looked vaguely familiar walked into the room and, waving a textbook in the air, said out loud, "Shall I sit alone and finish this book for the paper that is due tomorrow or shall I talk to someone?" That got my attention. I watched as she stood silently for a moment, then nodded, walked over to my table and sat down.

We began to chat and I realized that she had taken a course on grief and spirituality I had taught, a year previously. After about 20 minutes of getting caught up, she asked if I was writing another book. I told her about *God Detectives* and my hope to find a story about a sign from God. She sat silently for a moment or two and then said, "You can use my story about the eagle. It happened only last week." "The Sign" is Vivian's story, with virtually no edits at all.

In my work on spiritual discernment (decision-making in intentional partnership with God), adults and children frequently speak of God drawing their attention to a particular path or decision that is right for them. In the 16th century, Angela Merici, founder of the first teaching congregation of Christian women, said "For God has given free will to everyone, and therefore never forces anyone – but only calls, indicates, and persuades." Many spiritual writers and guides say that God is always inviting us to the path that will be for our greatest good. It is a life-long task to learn to hear and see God's touches in our lives.

God gets our attention and invites us to draw a particular meaning from an experience in order to help us in our lives. We may be drawn to a statement; or to a creature, such as the eagle; or to another person who speaks a message that is divinely inspired; and so on. Adults and kids often say that they know something is a sign from God when they experience a deep peace, a sense of rightness, a feeling of increased love, or other qualities associated with God.

Questions to consider with children

1. Have you ever had a feeling of rightness or peace or love just by being in a place?
2. Have you ever had a bad feeling in a place and known you had to leave it?
3. Do you get the chance to sit quietly and wonder?
4. Where do you go to feel closest to God?

7. What Can a Kid Do?

Jacob was strongly affected by hearing that children were involved in war. He experienced overwhelming pain and, in the quiet of a darkened room, he prayed. He asked Jesus for help and was receptive to God's response. He found that God heals us not necessarily by taking the pain away, but by giving us the strength, support, and courage we need to deal with life's realities. Not everyone will "hear" Jesus speak to them as Jacob did. However, many people tell of similar experiences they have had, especially as children. Often, there are no words attached to the message, but rather a sense of comfort. The person praying knows that God walks the path with them.

Many books about the Christian path speak of the importance of daily prayer. Among other benefits, prayer helps us deepen our faith and sustains us during times of trial. Marjorie Thompson, in her book *Family: The Forming Center*, discusses the value of daily prayer for each family member: "Authentic prayer, of necessity, changes us; there is simply no possibility of encountering the living God without being changed. Prayer demands that we acknowledge our limits and invite God's grace" (p. 74). For this type of prayer, we need to cultivate silence. Some people talk so much in prayer that they never give God an opening to respond.

Silence is hard! Many people – adults and children – become anxious with silence. We don't know what to do; we may worry we are being unproductive; we fill the prayer with words we think God wants to hear. Children, in turn, receive the message that silence is bad or wrong when they are so programmed with extracurricular activities that they have little or no time for "doing nothing." Ironically, they may also receive the message that silence is wrong when we encourage them to tell God their problems without also showing them how to simply *be* with God.

Space and time can be invaluable gifts to give a child. We can guard unscheduled time in their daily schedule. We can show them how we ourselves enjoy watching cloud patterns, listening to a bird's song, or just "being." We can teach children meditation, contemplative prayer, and other practices that will develop their ability to listen to the divine within. This quiet attentiveness can, at first, be held for just a few seconds. A little silence after saying grace at meals or after bedtime prayers lets adults, as well as children, know that prayer opens us to dialogue – not just monologue – with God.

"Wow, look at those colors!" said a child pointing at the sunset. Her mother nodded and replied, "They are too beautiful for words. Let's just sit quietly and drink the colors in." The two sat on the park bench for a short time in companionable silence, until something else caught the girl's attention. And they carried on.

Questions to consider with children

1. Why would Jacob be so sad at such a fun party?
2. Have you ever felt deeply sad?
3. Where do you go to be quiet?
4. Did Jesus fix the world?

About the Authors

Photo by Greg Johnson, Summerland, BC

Nancy Reeves and Linnea Good

Dr. Nancy Reeves is a clinical psychologist and spiritual director working in the area of trauma, grief, and loss with children and adults. She began her career as a preschool teacher and play therapist with young children. She has a BA in Child Care and an MA and PhD in Counseling Psychology. Currently, she is adjunct faculty in Educational Psychology and Leadership Studies at the University of Victoria and is in demand as a guest instructor at seminaries throughout Canada and the U.S. She is the author of the popular books *I'd Say Yes God, If I Knew What You Wanted* and *Found Through Loss: Healing stories from scripture and everyday sacredness.* She travels much of the year, conducting workshops and courses throughout North America, the U.K., Australia, and New Zealand. She is at www.NancyReeves.com.

Linnea Good is a singer-songwriter whose primary work is to help individuals and churches express their souls through music. She is a leader in the fields of music in worship, and all-ages worshipping together. Her background includes a BA in French Literature; a Master of Religious Education with a specialty in music as an educational tool; professional travels that have taken her to Europe, Australia, New Zealand, and the Middle East. The latest of her numerous CDs, *Swimmin' Like a Bird,* was thrice nominated for major Canadian awards as Outstanding Children's Album of the Year. She offers an Internet subscription for worship and music leaders, called the *Psalm-body's Prayin' Group.* She and drummer-spouse, David, share the joy and laundry of 3 children: Patrick, Nicole, and Isaac. She is found at www.LinneaGood.com.

About the Illustrator

Leslie Chevaliér is a lifelong artist and full-time mom, specializing in pen and ink work as well as portraits of people and animals. Her degree is in psychology and recreational therapy. She studied pastoral liturgy with children at Notre Dame University. She has spent her entire career working with children in varying capacities: mental health facilities, professional youth ministry, schools, and more. Wherever she has worked, she has shared her passion for arts and music. She lives in Ogden, Utah, with her husband, Dave, and two daughters, Shan and Scout. Her art is displayed at www.lesliealongthelines.net.

I, _____,

am an official God Detective!

God loves me and I love God!

God talks to people in many ways

I will listen and watch closely for God's messages

The "God Detectives" is an informal movement created by Dr. Nancy Reeves and Linnea Good. The goal of "God Detectives" is to foster young people's ability to discern the Holy Spirit in their lives, follow the teachings of Jesus more closely, and develop a deeper relationship with our Creator. Anyone can be a member regardless of age, race, or religious affiliation. There is no cost to join, nor membership requirement. For more information visit

www.goddetectives.com.